The Bremen Town Band

retold by Geof Smith
illustrated by John Hovell

Chapters

Harcourt

Orlando   Boston   Dallas   Chicago   San Diego

Visit *The Learning Site!*
www.harcourtschool.com

The Road to Bremen

Once there was a donkey that lived on a farm. For many years he quietly did hard work, pulling plows and carrying sacks of grain. Now he was getting older, and his knees hurt and his back ached when he carried weighty loads. He knew his owner was a thrifty man who couldn't afford to feed and keep an old donkey.

"What should I do?" the donkey wondered. "It won't be long before the farmer gets rid of me."

One day, he decided to run away. "I've always been fascinated by music," he said to himself. "I think I'll go to the bustling town of Bremen and join a band."

The next morning, before the sun was up, the donkey embarked on his journey. He had not been on the winding road for long when he met a dog lying in the grass. The dog's long, brown face rested between his paws, and he panted as if he'd just finished a marathon.

"Hello," the donkey said. "It's a chilly morning, but you seem very hot and tired. Is something wrong?"

"Oh . . . I am an old . . . dog," the dog replied between huffs and puffs. "I can no longer . . . keep up with my owner . . . when he hunts. What good is a hunting dog . . . that can't hunt? I have run away, but now . . . I don't have a job."

The donkey nodded. "I know how that feels. I'm off to join the Bremen Town Band. You're welcome to come with me."

The dog liked this idea very much, and he jumped up, his tail wagging, to join the donkey on the road to Bremen.

The air was warmer and the sun hung high in the blue sky when the two new friends met a cat. She slumped sadly on a tree stump by the road.

"What's the matter?" the donkey asked.

"Once I was able to catch all the mice in my lady's kitchen," the cat moaned, "but now I'm not so fast. I'm afraid my owner will get rid of me."

"Well, this is certainly your lucky day," the dog said. "We're off to join the Bremen Town Band. With such a melodious voice, I'm sure you would make a superb singer."

The cat thanked them for their generous offer. She purred with delight and then skipped off the stump to join the other hopeful musicians on the road.

The sun had slipped below the trees and the horizon was turning purple when the three friends met a rooster. He was walking in circles on the dusty road, holding his shaking head between his wings.

"What am I to do? What am I to do?" he mumbled to himself.

The donkey asked the rooster why he was so
upset. The rooster explained that the farmer who
kept him was planning a special dinner, and he was
afraid that he would be the main course!

"That's horrible," the donkey said, "but there's
no need to worry. You can come with us and join
the Bremen Town Band."

"Right," the cat meowed. "You also have a
melodious voice, so you can sing along with me."

The rooster puffed out his red chest, cock-a-
doodle-dooed proudly, and joined his fellow
musicians on the road to Bremen.

In the Forest

The donkey, the dog, the cat, and the rooster journeyed a while longer, until the sun was completely gone and the sky was dark. It had grown so dark, in fact, that they could barely see the road anymore.

"We're still a long way from Bremen," the donkey said, "and I don't think it's very safe to walk along this road in the dark. I suggest we stop and rest for the night."

Though they were hungry and a little cold, the others agreed. They wandered off the road and found a comfortable clearing in the woods. Soft leaves and pine needles blanketed the ground where the dog and the donkey rested. The cat and the rooster, however, curled up on cozy tree branches overhead.

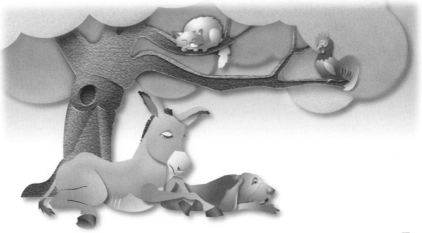

They were all settled when the cat, who was high up in the tree, called out to her friends, "Look! Over there! I see a light!"

The donkey jumped up and peered through the bushes. "Yes," he said, "I see it, too. Let's go find out what it is."

As they quietly crept closer, the light seemed to grow bigger and bigger, and soon the animals came to a small cabin. The glowing window looked into a kitchen.

"I bet it's very warm in front of the fireplace in that kitchen," the cat said.

The dog licked his lips and added, "I bet there's a delicious dinner on the table. We have to get closer."

Slowly the four animals tiptoed through the grass. Leaves rustled around them, and crickets chirped in the dark. The animals crept right up to the window. However, only the donkey was tall enough to see through the window.

"There are two men asleep inside," he whispered. "I see bread, cheese, and meat on the table."

"Let me see," the rooster said, and he fluttered onto the donkey's head.

"Oh, yes. There's a delightful soup bubbling in a pot on the fire," exclaimed the rooster. "It looks as if there's enough food to feed us for a month!"

"How I'd like to be in there," the dog said, and his stomach rumbled in agreement.

The four animals put their heads together and tried to think of a way to get inside so they could have some food. However, the dog cautioned them that if these men were anything like his old owner, they wouldn't enjoy being awakened by hungry, stray animals.

Actually, these two men were more wicked than any people the animals had ever known. These men were roguish thieves who were hiding from the police. They didn't want to see anyone that night, and they had no desire to share their food.

"I've got it," the donkey declared. "We're musicians, right? So let's earn our food with a performance. Okay?"

The others nodded in agreement. They all thought that this was the best possible approach. Each animal thought that singing was his or her strongest talent, and each one was eager to perform.

"We'll sing right here in front of this window," the donkey said. "I'm sure the audience will want to see us, so this is what we should do."

He used his hoof to draw in the dirt below the lighted window. "Dog, you can climb up on my back. Cat, you can get on the dog's shoulders. Rooster, you can perch on the cat at the very top."

The cat cleared her throat and sang a few notes. "I'm ready," she said.

11

Goblins, Monsters, and Dinner

As the animals climbed into position, they teetered and wobbled. The rooster held on tightly. The donkey's back hurt a little with the weight, but he was so grateful to be part of a band that he didn't care.

Then all of the animals started to sing. The donkey brayed, and the dog howled. The cat meowed, and the rooster crowed. It was truly a terrible sound.

The two men inside the cabin sprang up from the table. They were totally confused.

"What's that frightful noise?" they asked each other. "Where's it coming from?"

Suddenly, the donkey slipped.

CRASH!

Glass shattered as all the animals tumbled into the kitchen. The two terrified robbers leapt backward in fright. In the confusion, they were sure that a monster had come in through the broken window. The monster had feathers and fur and so many legs! What sort of monster could make such a hideous noise? The taller thief ran out the back door, and the smaller man screamed and followed him.

"Well," the donkey said, checking himself for injuries, "that certainly didn't go as planned."

"No," the dog replied, "but look at all that food!"

All four animals ate until their stomachs were so full that they could barely move. Finally, there was nothing they could do but sleep. The donkey rested in a pile of hay just outside the door while the cat curled up by the fire. The dog settled beneath a chair in a corner. The rooster flew up to a high shelf, perched there, and fell asleep.

It was a long time before the two robbers stopped running. When they did, they huffed and puffed until they caught their breath.

Finally, the taller one said, "What are we thinking? There are no monsters. Obviously some rascally thieves are trying to trick us. Go back to the cabin and find out what's going on."

The smaller thief wasn't happy, but he did go back
to the cabin . . . slowly. Carefully, he opened the door.
The kitchen was dark now, and everything was quiet.

The thief went to stoke the fire and accidentally
poked the cat. Naturally, the cat didn't like being
poked, so she jumped on his face, hissing and spitting.
The thief spun around and stepped on the dog's tail.
The dog growled and bit him on the leg. The thief's
yells woke up the rooster, who started crowing.

The robber ran for the door and tumbled into the
yard, where the donkey kicked him and sent him
flying. The robber scrambled up and ran off into the
night. He might have kept running forever if his friend
hadn't grabbed him and stopped him.

"Oh, it was horrifying!" the smaller thief cried.
"There is a frightening monster in that house. It must
have two mouths because it bit my face and chewed
my leg at the same time. It was so strong that with one
shove, it tossed me across the yard like a doll! As I ran
away, I heard it yelling, 'Catch the evildoer!' We have
to get away! I'm sure that monster is coming and
bringing its friends with it!"

The two thieves never returned to the cabin in the
woods, and the animals never reached Bremen.
Instead, the dog, the cat, the rooster, and, of course,
the donkey stayed in the house for a long time, and
every meal was hot and delicious.